A TRAMP ABROAD
Part 3
By Mark Twain
(Samuel L. Clemens)

CHAPTER XV
[Charming Waterside Pictures]

Men and women and cattle were at work in the dewy fields by this time. The people often stepped aboard the raft, as we glided along the grassy shores, and gossiped with us and with the crew for a hundred yards or so, then stepped ashore again, refreshed by the ride.

Only the men did this; the women were too busy. The women do all kinds of work on the continent. They dig, they hoe, they reap, they sow, they bear monstrous burdens on their backs, they shove similar ones long distances on wheelbarrows, they drag the cart when there is no dog or lean cow to drag it—and when there is, they assist the dog or cow. Age is no matter—the older the woman the stronger she is, apparently. On the farm a woman's duties are not defined—she does a little of everything; but in the towns it is different, there she only does certain things, the men do the rest. For instance, a hotel chambermaid has nothing to do but make beds and fires in fifty or sixty rooms, bring towels and candles, and fetch several tons of water up several flights of stairs, a hundred pounds at a time, in prodigious metal pitchers. She does not have to work more than eighteen or twenty hours a day, and she can always get down on her knees and scrub the floors of halls and closets when she is tired and needs a rest.

As the morning advanced and the weather grew hot, we took off our outside clothing and sat in a row along the edge of the raft and enjoyed the scenery, with our sun-umbrellas over our heads and our legs dangling in the water.

Every now and then we plunged in and had a swim. Every projecting grassy cape had its joyous group of naked children, the boys to themselves and the girls to themselves, the latter usually in care of some motherly dame who sat in the shade of a tree with her knitting. The little boys swam out to us, sometimes, but the little maids stood knee-deep in the water and stopped their splashing and frolicking to inspect the raft with their innocent eyes as it drifted by. Once we turned a corner suddenly and surprised a slender girl of twelve years or upward, just stepping into the water. She had not time to run, but she did what answered just as well; she promptly drew a lithe young willow bough athwart her white body with one hand, and then contemplated us with a simple and untroubled interest. Thus she stood while we glided by. She was a pretty creature, and she and her willow bough made a very pretty picture, and one which could not offend the modesty of the most fastidious spectator. Her white skin had a low bank of fresh green willows for background and effective contrast—for she stood against them—and above and out of them projected the eager faces and white shoulders of two smaller girls.

Toward noon we heard the inspiriting cry,—
"Sail ho!"
"Where away?" shouted the captain.

"Three points off the weather bow!"

We ran forward to see the vessel. It proved to be a steamboat—for they had begun to run a steamer up the Neckar, for the first time in May. She was a tug, and one of a very peculiar build and aspect. I had often watched her from the hotel, and wondered how she propelled herself, for apparently she had no propeller or paddles. She came churning along, now, making a deal of noise of one kind or another, and aggravating it every now and then by blowing a hoarse whistle. She had nine keel-boats hitched on behind and following after her in a long, slender rank. We met her in a narrow place, between dikes, and there was hardly room for us both in the cramped passage. As she went grinding and groaning by, we perceived the secret of her moving impulse. She did not drive herself up the river with paddles or propeller, she pulled herself by hauling on a great chain. This chain is laid in the bed of the river and is only fastened at the two ends. It is seventy miles long. It comes in over the boat's bow, passes around a drum, and is payed out astern. She pulls on that chain, and so drags herself up the river or down it. She has neither bow or stern, strictly speaking, for she has a long-bladed rudder on each end and she never turns around. She uses both rudders all the time, and they are powerful enough to enable her to turn to the right or the left and steer around curves, in spite of the strong resistance of the chain. I would not have believed that that impossible thing could be done; but I saw it done, and therefore I know that there is one impossible thing which CAN be done. What miracle will man attempt next?

We met many big keel-boats on their way up, using sails, mule power, and profanity—a tedious and laborious business. A wire rope led from the foretopmast to the file of mules on the tow-path a hundred yards ahead, and by dint of much banging and swearing and urging, the detachment of drivers managed to get a speed of two or three miles an hour out of the mules against the stiff current. The Neckar has always been used as a canal, and thus has given employment to a great many men and animals; but now that this steamboat is able, with a small crew and a bushel or so of coal, to take nine keel-boats farther up the river in one hour than thirty men and thirty mules can do it in two, it is believed that the old-fashioned towing industry is on its death-bed. A second steamboat began work in the Neckar three months after the first one was put in service. [Figure 4]

At noon we stepped ashore and bought some bottled beer and got some chickens cooked, while the raft waited; then we immediately put to sea again, and had our dinner while the beer was cold and the chickens hot. There is no pleasanter place for such a meal than a raft that is gliding down the winding Neckar past green meadows and wooded hills, and slumbering villages, and craggy heights graced with crumbling towers and battlements.

In one place we saw a nicely dressed German gentleman without any spectacles. Before I could come to anchor he had got underway. It was a great pity. I so wanted to make a sketch of him. The captain comforted me for my loss, however, by saying that the man was without any doubt a fraud who had spectacles, but kept them in his pocket in order to make himself conspicuous.

Below Hassmersheim we passed Hornberg, Goetz von Berlichingen's old castle. It stands on a bold elevation two hundred feet above the surface of the river; it has high vine-clad walls enclosing trees, and a peaked tower about seventy-five feet high. The steep hillside, from the castle clear down to the water's edge, is terraced, and clothed thick with grape vines. This is like farming a mansard roof. All the steeps along that part of the river which furnish the proper exposure, are given up to the grape. That region is a great producer of Rhine wines. The Germans are exceedingly fond of Rhine wines; they are put up in tall, slender bottles, and are considered a pleasant beverage. One tells them from vinegar by the label.

The Hornberg hill is to be tunneled, and the new railway will pass under the castle.

THE CAVE OF THE SPECTER

Two miles below Hornberg castle is a cave in a low cliff, which the captain of the raft said had once been occupied by a beautiful heiress of Hornberg—the Lady Gertrude—in the old times. It was seven hundred years ago. She had a number of rich and noble lovers and one poor and obscure one, Sir Wendel Lobenfeld. With the native chuckleheadedness of the heroine of romance, she preferred the poor and obscure lover.

With the native sound judgment of the father of a heroine of romance, the von Berlichingen of that day shut his daughter up in his donjon keep, or his oubliette, or his culverin, or some such place, and resolved that she should stay there until she selected a husband from among her rich and noble lovers. The latter visited her and persecuted her with their supplications, but without effect, for her heart was true to her poor despised Crusader, who was fighting in the Holy Land. Finally, she resolved that she would endure the attentions of the rich lovers no longer; so one stormy night she escaped and went down the river and hid herself in the cave on the other side. Her father ransacked the country for her, but found not a trace of her. As the days went by, and still no tidings of her came, his conscience began to torture him, and he caused proclamation to be made that if she were yet living and would return, he would oppose her no longer, she might marry whom she would. The months dragged on, all hope forsook the old man, he ceased from his customary pursuits and pleasures, he devoted himself to pious works, and longed for the deliverance of death.

Now just at midnight, every night, the lost heiress stood in the mouth of her cave, arrayed in white robes, and sang a little love ballad which her Crusader had made for her. She judged that if he came home alive the superstitious peasants would tell him about the ghost that sang in the cave, and that as soon as they described the ballad he would know that none but he and she knew that song, therefore he would suspect that she was alive, and would come and find her. As time went on, the people of the region became sorely distressed about the Specter of the Haunted Cave. It was said that ill luck of one kind or another always overtook any one who had the misfortune to hear that song. Eventually, every calamity that happened thereabouts was laid at the door of that music. Consequently, no boatmen would consent to pass the cave at night; the peasants shunned the place, even in the daytime.

But the faithful girl sang on, night after night, month after month, and patiently waited; her reward must come at last. Five years dragged by, and still, every night at midnight, the plaintive tones floated out over the silent land, while the distant boatmen and peasants thrust their fingers into their ears and shuddered out a prayer.

And now came the Crusader home, bronzed and battle-scarred, but bringing a great and splendid fame to lay at the feet of his bride. The old lord of Hornberg received him as his son, and wanted him to stay by him and be the comfort and blessing of his age; but the tale of that young girl's devotion to him and its pathetic consequences made a changed man of the knight. He could not enjoy his well-earned rest. He said his heart was broken, he would give the remnant of his life to high deeds in the cause of humanity, and so find a worthy death and a blessed reunion with the brave true heart whose love had more honored him than all his victories in war.

When the people heard this resolve of his, they came and told him there was a pitiless dragon in human disguise in the Haunted Cave, a dread creature which no knight had yet been bold enough to face, and begged him to rid the land of its desolating presence. He said he would do it. They told him about the song, and when he asked what song it was, they said the memory of it was gone, for nobody had been hardy enough to listen to it for the past four years and more.

Toward midnight the Crusader came floating down the river in a boat, with his trusty cross-bow in his hands. He drifted silently through the dim reflections of the crags and trees, with his intent eyes fixed upon the low cliff which he was approaching. As he drew nearer, he discerned the black mouth of the cave. Now—is that a white figure? Yes. The plaintive song begins to well forth and float away over meadow and river—the cross-bow is slowly raised to position, a steady aim is taken, the bolt flies straight to the mark—the figure sinks down, still singing, the knight takes the wool out of his ears, and recognizes the old ballad— too late! Ah, if he had only not put the wool in his ears!

The Crusader went away to the wars again, and presently fell in battle, fighting for the Cross. Tradition says that during several centuries the spirit of the unfortunate girl sang nightly from the cave at midnight, but the music carried no curse with it; and although many listened for the mysterious sounds, few were favored, since only those could hear them who had never failed in a trust. It is believed that the singing still continues, but it is known that nobody has heard it during the present century.

CHAPTER XVI
An Ancient Legend of the Rhine [The Lorelei]

The last legend reminds one of the "Lorelei"—a legend of the Rhine. There is a song called "The Lorelei."

Germany is rich in folk-songs, and the words and airs of several of them are peculiarly beautiful—but "The Lorelei" is the people's favorite. I could not endure it at first, but by and by it began to take hold of me, and now there is no tune which I like so well.

It is not possible that it is much known in America, else I should have heard it there. The fact that I never heard it there, is evidence that there are others in my country who have fared likewise; therefore, for the sake of these, I mean to print the words and music in this chapter. And I will refresh the reader's memory by printing the legend of the Lorelei, too. I have it by me in the LEGENDS OF THE RHINE, done into English by the wildly gifted Garnham, Bachelor of Arts. I print the legend partly to refresh my own memory, too, for I have never read it before.

THE LEGEND

Lore (two syllables) was a water nymph who used to sit on a high rock called the Ley or Lei (pronounced like our word LIE) in the Rhine, and lure boatmen to destruction in a furious rapid which marred the channel at that spot. She so bewitched them with her plaintive songs and her wonderful beauty that they forgot everything else to gaze up at her, and so they presently drifted among the broken reefs and were lost.

In those old, old times, the Count Bruno lived in a great castle near there with his son, the Count Hermann, a youth of twenty. Hermann had heard a great deal about the beautiful Lore, and had finally fallen very deeply in love with her without having seen her. So he used to wander to the neighborhood of the Lei, evenings, with his Zither and "Express his Longing in low Singing," as Garnham says. On one of these occasions, "suddenly there hovered around the top of the rock a brightness of unequaled clearness and color, which, in increasingly smaller circles thickened, was the enchanting figure of the beautiful Lore.

"An unintentional cry of Joy escaped the Youth, he let his Zither fall, and with extended arms he called out the name of the enigmatical Being, who seemed to stoop lovingly to him and beckon to him in a friendly manner; indeed, if his ear did not deceive him, she called his name with unutterable sweet Whispers, proper to love. Beside himself with delight the youth lost his Senses and sank senseless to the earth."

After that he was a changed person. He went dreaming about, thinking only of his fairy and caring for naught else in the world. "The old count saw with affliction this changement in his son," whose cause he could not divine, and tried to divert his mind into cheerful channels, but to no purpose. Then the old count used authority. He commanded the youth to betake himself to the camp. Obedience was promised. Garnham says:

"It was on the evening before his departure, as he wished still once to visit the Lei and offer to the Nymph of the Rhine his Sighs, the tones of his Zither, and his Songs. He went, in his boat, this time accompanied by a faithful squire, down the stream. The moon shed her silvery light over the whole country; the steep bank mountains appeared in the most fantastical shapes, and the high oaks on either side bowed their Branches on Hermann's passing. As soon as he approached the Lei, and was aware of the surf-waves, his attendant was seized with an inexpressible Anxiety and he begged permission to land; but the Knight swept the strings of his Guitar and sang:

> "Once I saw thee in dark night,
> In supernatural Beauty bright;
> Of Light-rays, was the Figure wove,
> To share its light, locked-hair strove.

"Thy Garment color wave-dove
By thy hand the sign of love,
Thy eyes sweet enchantment,
Raying to me, oh! enchantment.

"O, wert thou but my sweetheart,
How willingly thy love to part!
With delight I should be bound
To thy rocky house in deep ground."

That Hermann should have gone to that place at all, was not wise; that he should have gone with such a song as that in his mouth was a most serious mistake. The Lorelei did not "call his name in unutterable sweet Whispers" this time. No, that song naturally worked an instant and thorough "changement" in her; and not only that, but it stirred the bowels of the whole afflicted region around about there—for—

"Scarcely had these tones sounded, everywhere there began tumult and sound, as if voices above and below the water. On the Lei rose flames, the Fairy stood above, at that time, and beckoned with her right hand clearly and urgently to the infatuated Knight, while with a staff in her left hand she called the waves to her service. They began to mount heavenward; the boat was upset, mocking every exertion; the waves rose to the gunwale, and splitting on the hard stones, the Boat broke into Pieces. The youth sank into the depths, but the squire was thrown on shore by a powerful wave."

The bitterest things have been said about the Lorelei during many centuries, but surely her conduct upon this occasion entitles her to our respect. One feels drawn tenderly toward her and is moved to forget her many crimes and remember only the good deed that crowned and closed her career.

"The Fairy was never more seen; but her enchanting tones have often been heard. In the beautiful, refreshing, still nights of spring, when the moon pours her silver light over the Country, the listening shipper hears from the rushing of the waves, the echoing Clang of a wonderfully charming voice, which sings a song from the crystal castle, and with sorrow and fear he thinks on the young Count Hermann, seduced by the Nymph."

Here is the music, and the German words by Heinrich Heine. This song has been a favorite in Germany for forty years, and will remain a favorite always, maybe. [Figure 5]

I have a prejudice against people who print things in a foreign language and add no translation. When I am the reader, and the author considers me able to do the translating myself, he pays me quite a nice compliment—but if he would do the translating for me I would try to get along without the compliment.

If I were at home, no doubt I could get a translation of this poem, but I am abroad and can't; therefore I will make a translation myself. It may not be a good one, for poetry is out of my line, but it will serve my purpose—which is, to give the unGerman young girl a jingle of words to hang the tune on until she can get hold of a good version, made by some one who is a poet and knows how to convey a poetical thought from one language to another.

THE LORELEI

I cannot divine what it meaneth,

This haunting nameless pain:
A tale of the bygone ages
Keeps brooding through my brain:

The faint air cools in the glooming,
And peaceful flows the Rhine,
The thirsty summits are drinking
The sunset's flooding wine;

The loveliest maiden is sitting
High-throned in yon blue air,
Her golden jewels are shining,
She combs her golden hair;

She combs with a comb that is golden,
And sings a weird refrain
That steeps in a deadly enchantment
The list'ner's ravished brain:

The doomed in his drifting shallop,
Is tranced with the sad sweet tone,
He sees not the yawning breakers,
He sees but the maid alone:

The pitiless billows engulf him!—
So perish sailor and bark;
And this, with her baleful singing,
Is the Lorelei's gruesome work.

I have a translation by Garnham, Bachelor of Arts, in the LEGENDS OF THE RHINE, but it would not answer the purpose I mentioned above, because the measure is too nobly irregular; it don't fit the tune snugly enough; in places it hangs over at the ends too far, and in other places one runs out of words before he gets to the end of a bar. Still, Garnham's translation has high merits, and I am not dreaming of leaving it out of my book. I believe this poet is wholly unknown in America and England; I take peculiar pleasure in bringing him forward because I consider that I discovered him:

THE LORELEI

Translated by L. W. Garnham, B.A.

I do not know what it signifies.
That I am so sorrowful?
A fable of old Times so terrifies,
Leaves my heart so thoughtful.

The air is cool and it darkens,
And calmly flows the Rhine;
The summit of the mountain hearkens
In evening sunshine line.

> The most beautiful Maiden entrances
> Above wonderfully there,
> Her beautiful golden attire glances,
> She combs her golden hair.
>
> With golden comb so lustrous,
> And thereby a song sings,
> It has a tone so wondrous,
> That powerful melody rings.
>
> The shipper in the little ship
> It effects with woe sad might;
> He does not see the rocky slip,
> He only regards dreaded height.
>
> I believe the turbulent waves
> Swallow the last shipper and boat;
> She with her singing craves
> All to visit hermagic moat.

No translation could be closer. He has got in all the facts; and in their regular order, too. There is not a statistic wanting. It is as succinct as an invoice. That is what a translation ought to be; it should exactly reflect the thought of the original. You can't SING "Above wonderfully there," because it simply won't go to the tune, without damaging the singer; but it is a most clingingly exact translation of DORT OBEN WUNDERBAR—fits it like a blister. Mr. Garnham's reproduction has other merits—a hundred of them—but it is not necessary to point them out. They will be detected.

No one with a specialty can hope to have a monopoly of it. Even Garnham has a rival. Mr. X had a small pamphlet with him which he had bought while on a visit to Munich. It was entitled A CATALOGUE OF PICTURES IN THE OLD PINACOTEK, and was written in a peculiar kind of English. Here are a few extracts:

"It is not permitted to make use of the work in question to a publication of the same contents as well as to the pirated edition of it."

"An evening landscape. In the foreground near a pond and a group of white beeches is leading a footpath animated by travelers."

"A learned man in a cynical and torn dress holding an open book in his hand."

"St. Bartholomew and the Executioner with the knife to fulfil the martyr."

"Portrait of a young man. A long while this picture was thought to be Bindi Altoviti's portrait; now somebody will again have it to be the self-portrait of Raphael."

"Susan bathing, surprised by the two old man. In the background the lapidation of the condemned."

("Lapidation" is good; it is much more elegant than "stoning.")

"St. Rochus sitting in a landscape with an angel who looks at his plague-sore, whilst the dog the bread in his mouth attents him."

"Spring. The Goddess Flora, sitting. Behind her a fertile valley perfused by a river."

"A beautiful bouquet animated by May-bugs, etc."

"A warrior in armor with a gypseous pipe in his hand leans against a table and blows the smoke far away of himself."

"A Dutch landscape along a navigable river which perfuses it till to the background."

"Some peasants singing in a cottage. A woman lets drink a child out of a cup."

"St. John's head as a boy—painted in fresco on a brick." (Meaning a tile.)

"A young man of the Riccio family, his hair cut off right at the end, dressed in black with the same cap. Attributed to Raphael, but the signation is false."

"The Virgin holding the Infant. It is very painted in the manner of Sassoferrato."

"A Larder with greens and dead game animated by a cook-maid and two kitchen-boys."

However, the English of this catalogue is at least as happy as that which distinguishes an inscription upon a certain picture in Rome—to wit:

"Revelations-View. St. John in Patterson's Island."

But meanwhile the raft is moving on.

CHAPTER XVII
[Why Germans Wear Spectacles]

A mile or two above Eberbach we saw a peculiar ruin projecting above the foliage which clothed the peak of a high and very steep hill. This ruin consisted of merely a couple of crumbling masses of masonry which bore a rude resemblance to human faces; they leaned forward and touched foreheads, and had the look of being absorbed in conversation. This ruin had nothing very imposing or picturesque about it, and there was no great deal of it, yet it was called the "Spectacular Ruin."

LEGEND OF THE "SPECTACULAR RUIN"

The captain of the raft, who was as full of history as he could stick, said that in the Middle Ages a most prodigious fire-breathing dragon used to live in that region, and made more trouble than a tax-collector. He was as long as a railway-train, and had the customary impenetrable green scales all over him. His breath bred pestilence and conflagration, and his appetite bred famine. He ate men and cattle impartially, and was exceedingly unpopular. The German emperor of that day made the usual offer: he would grant to the destroyer of the dragon, any one solitary thing he might ask for; for he had a surplusage of daughters, and it was customary for dragon-killers to take a daughter for pay.

So the most renowned knights came from the four corners of the earth and retired down the dragon's throat one after the other. A panic arose and spread. Heroes grew cautious. The procession ceased. The dragon became more destructive than ever. The people lost all hope of succor, and fled to the mountains for refuge.

At last Sir Wissenschaft, a poor and obscure knight, out of a far country, arrived to do battle with the monster. A pitiable object he was, with his armor hanging in rags about him, and his strange-shaped knapsack strapped upon his back. Everybody turned up their noses at him, and some openly jeered him. But he was calm. He simply inquired if the emperor's offer was still in force. The emperor said it was—but charitably advised him to go and hunt hares and not endanger so precious a life as his in an attempt which had brought death to so many of the world's most illustrious heroes.

But this tramp only asked—"Were any of these heroes men of science?" This raised a laugh, of course, for science was despised in those days. But the tramp was not in the least ruffled. He said he might be a little in advance of his age, but no matter—science would come to be honored, some time or other. He said he would march against the dragon in the morning. Out of compassion, then, a decent spear was offered him, but he declined, and said, "spears were useless to men of science." They allowed him to sup in the servants' hall, and gave him a bed in the stables.

When he started forth in the morning, thousands were gathered to see. The emperor said:

"Do not be rash, take a spear, and leave off your knapsack."

But the tramp said:

"It is not a knapsack," and moved straight on.

The dragon was waiting and ready. He was breathing forth vast volumes of sulphurous smoke and lurid blasts of flame. The ragged knight stole warily to a good position, then he unslung his cylindrical knapsack—which was simply the common fire-extinguisher known to modern times—and the first chance he got he turned on his hose and shot the dragon square in the center of his cavernous mouth. Out went the fires in an instant, and the dragon curled up and died.

This man had brought brains to his aid. He had reared dragons from the egg, in his laboratory, he had watched over them like a mother, and patiently studied them and experimented upon them while they grew. Thus he had found out that fire was the life principle of a dragon; put out the dragon's fires and it could make steam no longer, and must die. He could not put out a fire with a spear, therefore he invented the extinguisher. The dragon being dead, the emperor fell on the hero's neck and said:

"Deliverer, name your request," at the same time beckoning out behind with his heel for a detachment of his daughters to form and advance. But the tramp gave them no observance. He simply said:

"My request is, that upon me be conferred the monopoly of the manufacture and sale of spectacles in Germany."

The emperor sprang aside and exclaimed:

"This transcends all the impudence I ever heard! A modest demand, by my halidome! Why didn't you ask for the imperial revenues at once, and be done with it?"

But the monarch had given his word, and he kept it. To everybody's surprise, the unselfish monopolist immediately reduced the price of spectacles to such a degree that a great and crushing burden was removed from the nation. The emperor, to commemorate this generous act, and to testify his appreciation of it, issued a decree commanding everybody to buy this benefactor's spectacles and wear them, whether they needed them or not.

So originated the wide-spread custom of wearing spectacles in Germany; and as a custom once established in these old lands is imperishable, this one remains universal in the empire to this day. Such is the legend of the monopolist's once stately and sumptuous castle, now called the "Spectacular Ruin."

On the right bank, two or three miles below the Spectacular Ruin, we passed by a noble pile of castellated buildings overlooking the water from the crest of a lofty elevation. A stretch of two hundred yards of the high front wall was heavily draped with ivy, and out of the mass of buildings within rose three picturesque old towers. The place was in fine order, and was inhabited by a family of princely rank. This castle had its legend, too, but I should not feel justified in repeating it because I doubted the truth of some of its minor details.

Along in this region a multitude of Italian laborers were blasting away the frontage of the hills to make room for the new railway. They were fifty or a hundred feet above the river. As we turned a sharp corner they began to wave signals and shout warnings to us to look out for the explosions. It was all very well to warn us, but what could WE do? You can't back a raft upstream, you can't hurry it downstream, you can't scatter out to one side when you haven't any room to speak of, you won't take to the perpendicular cliffs on the other shore when they appear to be blasting there, too. Your resources are limited, you see. There is simply nothing for it but to watch and pray.

For some hours we had been making three and a half or four miles an hour and we were still making that. We had been dancing right along until those men began to shout; then for the next ten minutes it seemed to me that I had never seen a raft go so slowly. When the first blast went off we raised our sun-umbrellas and waited for the result. No harm done; none of the stones fell in the water. Another blast followed, and another and another. Some of the rubbish fell in the water just astern of us.

We ran that whole battery of nine blasts in a row, and it was certainly one of the most exciting and uncomfortable weeks I ever spent, either aship or ashore. Of course we frequently manned the poles and shoved earnestly for a second or so, but every time one of those spurts of dust and debris shot aloft every man dropped his pole and looked up to get the bearings of his share of it. It was very busy times along there for a while. It appeared certain that we must perish, but even that was not the bitterest thought; no, the abjectly unheroic nature of the death—that was the sting—that and the bizarre wording of the resulting obituary: "SHOT WITH A ROCK, ON A RAFT." There would be no poetry written about it. None COULD be written about it. Example:

NOT by war's shock, or war's shaft,—SHOT, with a rock, on a raft.

No poet who valued his reputation would touch such a theme as that. I should be distinguished as the only "distinguished dead" who went down to the grave unsonneted, in 1878.

But we escaped, and I have never regretted it. The last blast was a peculiarly strong one, and after the small rubbish was done raining around us and we were just going to shake hands over our deliverance, a later and larger stone came down amongst our little group of pedestrians and wrecked an umbrella. It did no other harm, but we took to the water just the same.

It seems that the heavy work in the quarries and the new railway gradings is done mainly by Italians. That was a revelation. We have the notion in our country that Italians never do heavy work at all, but confine themselves to the lighter arts, like organ-grinding, operatic singing, and assassination. We have blundered, that is plain.

All along the river, near every village, we saw little station-houses for the future railway. They were finished and waiting for the rails and business. They were as trim and snug and pretty as they could be. They were always of brick or stone; they were of graceful shape, they had vines and flowers about them already, and around them the grass was bright and green, and showed that it was carefully looked after. They were a decoration to the beautiful landscape, not an offense. Wherever one saw a pile of gravel or a pile of broken stone, it was always heaped as trimly and exactly as a new grave or a stack of cannon-balls; nothing about those stations or along the railroad or the wagon-road was allowed to look shabby or be unornamental. The keeping a country in such beautiful order as Germany exhibits, has a wise practical side to it, too, for it keeps thousands of people in work and bread who would otherwise be idle and mischievous.

As the night shut down, the captain wanted to tie up, but I thought maybe we might make Hirschhorn, so we went on. Presently the sky became overcast, and the captain came aft looking uneasy. He cast his eye aloft, then shook his head, and said it was coming on to blow. My party wanted to land at once—therefore I wanted to go on. The captain said we ought to shorten sail anyway, out of common prudence. Consequently, the larboard watch was ordered to lay in his pole. It grew quite dark, now, and the wind began to rise. It wailed through the swaying branches of the trees, and swept our decks in fitful gusts. Things were taking on an ugly look. The captain shouted to the steersman on the forward log:

"How's she landing?"

The answer came faint and hoarse from far forward:

"Nor'-east-and-by-nor'—east-by-east, half-east, sir."

"Let her go off a point!"

"Aye-aye, sir!"

"What water have you got?"

"Shoal, sir. Two foot large, on the stabboard, two and a half scant on the labboard!"

"Let her go off another point!"

"Aye-aye, sir!"

"Forward, men, all of you! Lively, now! Stand by to crowd her round the weather corner!"

"Aye-aye, sir!"

Then followed a wild running and trampling and hoarse shouting, but the forms of the men were lost in the darkness and the sounds were distorted and confused by the roaring of the wind through the shingle-bundles. By this time the sea was running inches high, and threatening every moment to engulf the frail bark. Now came the mate, hurrying aft, and said, close to the captain's ear, in a low, agitated voice:

"Prepare for the worst, sir—we have sprung a leak!"

"Heavens! where?"

"Right aft the second row of logs."

"Nothing but a miracle can save us! Don't let the men know, or there will be a panic and mutiny! Lay her in shore and stand by to jump with the stern-line the moment she touches. Gentlemen, I must look to you to second my endeavors in this hour of peril. You have hats—go forward and bail for your lives!"

Down swept another mighty blast of wind, clothed in spray and thick darkness. At such a moment as this, came from away forward that most appalling of all cries that are ever heard at sea:

"MAN OVERBOARD!"

The captain shouted:

"Hard a-port! Never mind the man! Let him climb aboard or wade ashore!"

Another cry came down the wind:

"Breakers ahead!"

"Where away?"

"Not a log's length off her port fore-foot!"

We had groped our slippery way forward, and were now bailing with the frenzy of despair, when we heard the mate's terrified cry, from far aft:

"Stop that dashed bailing, or we shall be aground!"

But this was immediately followed by the glad shout:

"Land aboard the starboard transom!"

"Saved!" cried the captain. "Jump ashore and take a turn around a tree and pass the bight aboard!"

The next moment we were all on shore weeping and embracing for joy, while the rain poured down in torrents. The captain said he had been a mariner for forty years on the Neckar, and in that time had seen storms to make a man's cheek blanch and his pulses stop, but he had never, never seen a storm that even approached this one. How familiar that sounded! For I have been at sea a good deal and have heard that remark from captains with a frequency accordingly.

We framed in our minds the usual resolution of thanks and admiration and gratitude, and took the first opportunity to vote it, and put it in writing and present it to the captain, with the customary speech. We tramped through the darkness and the drenching summer rain full three miles, and reached "The Naturalist Tavern" in the village of Hirschhorn just an hour before midnight, almost exhausted from hardship, fatigue, and terror. I can never forget that night.

The landlord was rich, and therefore could afford to be crusty and disobliging; he did not at all like being turned out of his warm bed to open his house for us. But no matter, his household got up and cooked a quick supper for us, and we brewed a hot punch for ourselves, to keep off consumption. After supper and punch we had an hour's soothing smoke while we fought the naval battle over again and voted the resolutions; then we retired to exceedingly neat and pretty chambers upstairs that had clean, comfortable beds in them with heirloom pillowcases most elaborately and tastefully embroidered by hand.

Such rooms and beds and embroidered linen are as frequent in German village inns as they are rare in ours. Our villages are superior to German villages in more merits, excellences, conveniences, and privileges than I can enumerate, but the hotels do not belong in the list.

"The Naturalist Tavern" was not a meaningless name; for all the halls and all the rooms were lined with large glass cases which were filled with all sorts of birds and animals, glass-eyed, ably stuffed, and set up in the most natural eloquent and dramatic attitudes. The moment we were abed, the rain cleared away and the moon came out. I dozed off to sleep while contemplating a great white stuffed owl which was looking intently down on me from a high perch with the air of a person who thought he had met me before, but could not make out for certain.

But young Z did not get off so easily. He said that as he was sinking deliciously to sleep, the moon lifted away the shadows and developed a huge cat, on a bracket, dead and stuffed, but crouching, with every muscle tense, for a spring, and with its glittering glass eyes aimed straight at him. It made Z uncomfortable. He tried closing his own eyes, but that did not answer, for a natural instinct kept making him open them again to see if the cat was still getting ready to launch at him—which she always was. He tried turning his back, but that was a failure; he knew the sinister eyes were on him still. So at last he had to get up, after an hour or two of worry and experiment, and set the cat out in the hall. So he won, that time.

CHAPTER XVIII
[The Kindly Courtesy of Germans]

In the morning we took breakfast in the garden, under the trees, in the delightful German summer fashion. The air was filled with the fragrance of flowers and wild animals; the living portion of the menagerie of the "Naturalist Tavern" was all about us. There were great cages populous with fluttering and chattering foreign birds, and other great cages and greater wire pens, populous with quadrupeds, both native and foreign. There were some free creatures, too, and quite sociable ones they were. White rabbits went loping about the place, and occasionally came and sniffed at our shoes and shins; a fawn, with a red ribbon on its neck, walked up and examined us fearlessly; rare breeds of chickens and doves begged for crumbs, and a poor old tailless raven hopped about with a humble, shamefaced mein which said, "Please do not notice my exposure—think how you would feel in my circumstances, and be charitable." If he was observed too much, he would retire behind something and stay there until he judged the party's interest had found another object. I never have seen another dumb creature that was so morbidly sensitive. Bayard Taylor, who could interpret the dim reasonings of animals, and understood their moral natures better than most men, would have found some way to make this poor old chap forget his troubles for a while, but we have not his kindly art, and so had to leave the raven to his griefs.

After breakfast we climbed the hill and visited the ancient castle of Hirschhorn, and the ruined church near it. There were some curious old bas-reliefs leaning against the inner walls of the church—sculptured lords of Hirschhorn in complete armor, and ladies of Hirschhorn in the picturesque court costumes of the Middle Ages. These things are suffering damage and passing to decay, for the last Hirschhorn has been dead two hundred years, and there is nobody now who cares to preserve the family relics. In the chancel was a twisted stone column, and the captain told us a legend about it, of course, for in the matter of legends he could not seem to restrain himself; but I do not repeat his tale because there was nothing plausible about it except that the Hero wrenched this column into its present screw-shape with his hands —just one single wrench. All the rest of the legend was doubtful.

But Hirschhorn is best seen from a distance, down the river. Then the clustered brown towers perched on the green hilltop, and the old battlemented stone wall, stretching up and over the grassy ridge and disappearing in the leafy sea beyond, make a picture whose grace and beauty entirely satisfy the eye.

We descended from the church by steep stone stairways which curved this way and that down narrow alleys between the packed and dirty tenements of the village. It was a quarter well stocked with deformed, leering, unkempt and uncombed idiots, who held out hands or caps and begged piteously. The people of the quarter were not all idiots, of course, but all that begged seemed to be, and were said to be.

I was thinking of going by skiff to the next town, Necharsteinach; so I ran to the riverside in advance of the party and asked a man there if he had a boat to hire. I suppose I must have spoken High German—Court German—I intended it for that, anyway—so he did not understand me. I turned and twisted my question around and about, trying to strike that man's average, but failed. He could not make out what I wanted. Now Mr. X arrived, faced this same man, looked him in the eye, and emptied this sentence on him, in the most glib and confident way: "Can man boat get here?"

The mariner promptly understood and promptly answered. I can comprehend why he was able to understand that particular sentence, because by mere accident all the words in it except "get" have the same sound and the same meaning in German that they have in English; but how he managed to understand Mr. X's next remark puzzled me. I will insert it, presently. X turned away a moment, and asked the mariner if he could not find a board, and so construct an additional seat. I spoke in the purest German, but I might as well have spoken in the purest Choctaw for all the good it did. The man tried his best to understand me; he tried, and kept on trying, harder and harder, until I saw it was really of no use, and said:

"There, don't strain yourself—it is of no consequence."

Then X turned to him and crisply said:

"MACHEN SIE a flat board."

I wish my epitaph may tell the truth about me if the man did not answer up at once, and say he would go and borrow a board as soon as he had lit the pipe which he was filling.

We changed our mind about taking a boat, so we did not have to go. I have given Mr. X's two remarks just as he made them. Four of the five words in the first one were English, and that they were also German was only accidental, not intentional; three out of the five words in the second remark were English, and English only, and the two German ones did not mean anything in particular, in such a connection.

X always spoke English to Germans, but his plan was to turn the sentence wrong end first and upside down, according to German construction, and sprinkle in a German word without any essential meaning to it, here and there, by way of flavor. Yet he always made himself understood. He could make those dialect-speaking raftsmen understand him, sometimes, when even young Z had failed with them; and young Z was a pretty good German scholar. For one thing, X always spoke with such confidence—perhaps that helped. And possibly the raftsmen's dialect was what is called PLATT-DEUTSCH, and so they found his English more familiar to their ears than another man's German. Quite indifferent students of German can read Fritz Reuter's charming platt-Deutch tales with some little facility because many of the words are English. I suppose this is the tongue which our Saxon ancestors carried to England with them. By and by I will inquire of some other philologist.

However, in the mean time it had transpired that the men employed to calk the raft had found that the leak was not a leak at all, but only a crack between the logs—a crack that belonged there, and was not dangerous, but had been magnified into a leak by the disordered imagination of the mate. Therefore we went aboard again with a good degree of confidence, and presently got to sea without accident. As we swam smoothly along between the enchanting shores, we fell to swapping notes about manners and customs in Germany and elsewhere.

As I write, now, many months later, I perceive that each of us, by observing and noting and inquiring, diligently and day by day, had managed to lay in a most varied and opulent stock of misinformation. But this is not surprising; it is very difficult to get accurate details in any country. For example, I had the idea once, in Heidelberg, to find out all about those five student-corps. I started with the White Cap corps. I began to inquire of this and that and the other citizen, and here is what I found out:

1. It is called the Prussian Corps, because none but Prussians are admitted to it.

2. It is called the Prussian Corps for no particular reason. It has simply pleased each corps to name itself after some German state.

3. It is not named the Prussian Corps at all, but only the White Cap Corps.
4. Any student can belong to it who is a German by birth.
5. Any student can belong to it who is European by birth.
6. Any European-born student can belong to it, except he be a Frenchman.
7. Any student can belong to it, no matter where he was born.
8. No student can belong to it who is not of noble blood.
9. No student can belong to it who cannot show three full generations of noble descent.
10. Nobility is not a necessary qualification.
11. No moneyless student can belong to it.
12. Money qualification is nonsense—such a thing has never been thought of.

I got some of this information from students themselves—students who did not belong to the corps.

I finally went to headquarters—to the White Caps—where I would have gone in the first place if I had been acquainted. But even at headquarters I found difficulties; I perceived that there were things about the White Cap Corps which one member knew and another one didn't. It was natural; for very few members of any organization know ALL that can be known about it. I doubt there is a man or a woman in Heidelberg who would not answer promptly and confidently three out of every five questions about the White Cap Corps which a stranger might ask; yet it is a very safe bet that two of the three answers would be incorrect every time.

There is one German custom which is universal—the bowing courteously to strangers when sitting down at table or rising up from it. This bow startles a stranger out of his self-possession, the first time it occurs, and he is likely to fall over a chair or something, in his embarrassment, but it pleases him, nevertheless. One soon learns to expect this bow and be on the lookout and ready to return it; but to learn to lead off and make the initial bow one's self is a difficult matter for a diffident man. One thinks, "If I rise to go, and tender my bow, and these ladies and gentlemen take it into their heads to ignore the custom of their nation, and not return it, how shall I feel, in case I survive to feel anything." Therefore he is afraid to venture. He sits out the dinner, and makes the strangers rise first and originate the bowing. A table d'hôte dinner is a tedious affair for a man who seldom touches anything after the three first courses; therefore I used to do some pretty dreary waiting because of my fears. It took me months to assure myself that those fears were groundless, but I did assure myself at last by experimenting diligently through my agent. I made Harris get up and bow and leave; invariably his bow was returned, then I got up and bowed myself and retired.

Thus my education proceeded easily and comfortably for me, but not for Harris. Three courses of a table d'hôte dinner were enough for me, but Harris preferred thirteen.

Even after I had acquired full confidence, and no longer needed the agent's help, I sometimes encountered difficulties. Once at Baden-Baden I nearly lost a train because I could not be sure that three young ladies opposite me at table were Germans, since I had not heard them speak; they might be American, they might be English, it was not safe to venture a bow; but just as I had got that far with my thought, one of them began a German remark, to my great relief and gratitude; and before she got out her third word, our bows had been delivered and graciously returned, and we were off.

There is a friendly something about the German character which is very winning. When Harris and I were making a pedestrian tour through the Black Forest, we stopped at a little country inn for dinner one day; two young ladies and a young gentleman entered and sat down opposite us. They were pedestrians, too. Our knapsacks were strapped upon our backs, but they had a sturdy youth along to carry theirs for them. All parties were hungry, so there was no talking. By and by the usual bows were exchanged, and we separated.

As we sat at a late breakfast in the hotel at Allerheiligen, next morning, these young people entered and took places near us without observing us; but presently they saw us and at once bowed and smiled; not ceremoniously, but with the gratified look of people who have found acquaintances where they were expecting strangers. Then they spoke of the weather and the roads. We also spoke of the weather and the roads. Next, they said they had had an enjoyable walk, notwithstanding the weather. We said that that had been our case, too. Then they said they had walked thirty English miles the day before, and asked how many we had walked. I could not lie, so I told Harris to do it. Harris told them we had made thirty English miles, too. That was true; we had "made" them, though we had had a little assistance here and there.

After breakfast they found us trying to blast some information out of the dumb hotel clerk about routes, and observing that we were not succeeding pretty well, they went and got their maps and things, and pointed out and explained our course so clearly that even a New York detective could have followed it. And when we started they spoke out a hearty good-by and wished us a pleasant journey. Perhaps they were more generous with us than they might have been with native wayfarers because we were a forlorn lot and in a strange land; I don't know; I only know it was lovely to be treated so.

Very well, I took an American young lady to one of the fine balls in Baden-Baden, one night, and at the entrance-door upstairs we were halted by an official—something about Miss Jones's dress was not according to rule; I don't remember what it was, now; something was wanting—her back hair, or a shawl, or a fan, or a shovel, or something. The official was ever so polite, and ever so sorry, but the rule was strict, and he could not let us in. It was very embarrassing, for many eyes were on us. But now a richly dressed girl stepped out of the ballroom, inquired into the trouble, and said she could fix it in a moment. She took Miss Jones to the robing-room, and soon brought her back in regulation trim, and then we entered the ballroom with this benefactress unchallenged.

Being safe, now, I began to puzzle through my sincere but ungrammatical thanks, when there was a sudden mutual recognition —the benefactress and I had met at Allerheiligen. Two weeks had not altered her good face, and plainly her heart was in the right place yet, but there was such a difference between these clothes and the clothes I had seen her in before, when she was walking thirty miles a day in the Black Forest, that it was quite natural that I had failed to recognize her sooner. I had on MY other suit, too, but my German would betray me to a person who had heard it once, anyway. She brought her brother and sister, and they made our way smooth for that evening.

Well—months afterward, I was driving through the streets of Munich in a cab with a German lady, one day, when she said:

"There, that is Prince Ludwig and his wife, walking along there."

Everybody was bowing to them—cabmen, little children, and everybody else—and they were returning all the bows and overlooking nobody, when a young lady met them and made a deep courtesy.

"That is probably one of the ladies of the court," said my German friend.

I said:

"She is an honor to it, then. I know her. I don't know her name, but I know HER. I have known her at Allerheiligen and Baden-Baden. She ought to be an Empress, but she may be only a Duchess; it is the way things go in this way."

17

If one asks a German a civil question, he will be quite sure to get a civil answer. If you stop a German in the street and ask him to direct you to a certain place, he shows no sign of feeling offended. If the place be difficult to find, ten to one the man will drop his own matters and go with you and show you.

In London, too, many a time, strangers have walked several blocks with me to show me my way.

There is something very real about this sort of politeness. Quite often, in Germany, shopkeepers who could not furnish me the article I wanted have sent one of their employees with me to show me a place where it could be had.

CHAPTER XIX
[The Deadly Jest of Dilsberg]

However, I wander from the raft. We made the port of Necharsteinach in good season, and went to the hotel and ordered a trout dinner, the same to be ready against our return from a two-hour pedestrian excursion to the village and castle of Dilsberg, a mile distant, on the other side of the river. I do not mean that we proposed to be two hours making two miles—no, we meant to employ most of the time in inspecting Dilsberg.

For Dilsberg is a quaint place. It is most quaintly and picturesquely situated, too. Imagine the beautiful river before you; then a few rods of brilliant green sward on its opposite shore; then a sudden hill—no preparatory gently rising slopes, but a sort of instantaneous hill—a hill two hundred and fifty or three hundred feet high, as round as a bowl, with the same taper upward that an inverted bowl has, and with about the same relation of height to diameter that distinguishes a bowl of good honest depth—a hill which is thickly clothed with green bushes—a comely, shapely hill, rising abruptly out of the dead level of the surrounding green plains, visible from a great distance down the bends of the river, and with just exactly room on the top of its head for its steepled and turreted and roof-clustered cap of architecture, which same is tightly jammed and compacted within the perfectly round hoop of the ancient village wall.

There is no house outside the wall on the whole hill, or any vestige of a former house; all the houses are inside the wall, but there isn't room for another one. It is really a finished town, and has been finished a very long time. There is no space between the wall and the first circle of buildings; no, the village wall is itself the rear wall of the first circle of buildings, and the roofs jut a little over the wall and thus furnish it with eaves. The general level of the massed roofs is gracefully broken and relieved by the dominating towers of the ruined castle and the tall spires of a couple of churches; so, from a distance Dilsberg has rather more the look of a king's crown than a cap. That lofty green eminence and its quaint coronet form quite a striking picture, you may be sure, in the flush of the evening sun.

We crossed over in a boat and began the ascent by a narrow, steep path which plunged us at once into the leafy deeps of the bushes. But they were not cool deeps by any means, for the sun's rays were weltering hot and there was little or no breeze to temper them. As we panted up the sharp ascent, we met brown, bareheaded and barefooted boys and girls, occasionally, and sometimes men; they came upon us without warning, they gave us good day, flashed out of sight in the bushes, and were gone as suddenly and mysteriously as they had come. They were bound for the other side of the river to work. This path had been traveled by many generations of these people. They have always gone down to the valley to earn their bread, but they have always climbed their hill again to eat it, and to sleep in their snug town.

It is said that the Dilsbergers do not emigrate much; they find that living up there above the world, in their peaceful nest, is pleasanter than living down in the troublous world. The seven hundred inhabitants are all blood-kin to each other, too; they have always been blood-kin to each other for fifteen hundred years; they are simply one large family, and they like the home folks better than they like strangers, hence they persistently stay at home. It has been said that for ages Dilsberg has been merely a thriving and diligent idiot-factory. I saw no idiots there, but the captain said, "Because of late years the government has taken to lugging them off to asylums and otherwheres; and government wants to cripple the factory, too, and is trying to get these Dilsbergers to marry out of the family, but they don't like to."

The captain probably imagined all this, as modern science denies that the intermarrying of relatives deteriorates the stock.

Arrived within the wall, we found the usual village sights and life. We moved along a narrow, crooked lane which had been paved in the Middle Ages. A strapping, ruddy girl was beating flax or some such stuff in a little bit of a good-box of a barn, and she swung her flail with a will—if it was a flail; I was not farmer enough to know what she was at; a frowsy, barelegged girl was herding half a dozen geese with a stick—driving them along the lane and keeping them out of the dwellings; a cooper was at work in a shop which I know he did not make so large a thing as a hogshead in, for there was not room. In the front rooms of dwellings girls and women were cooking or spinning, and ducks and chickens were waddling in and out, over the threshold, picking up chance crumbs and holding pleasant converse; a very old and wrinkled man sat asleep before his door, with his chin upon his breast and his extinguished pipe in his lap; soiled children were playing in the dirt everywhere along the lane, unmindful of the sun.

Except the sleeping old man, everybody was at work, but the place was very still and peaceful, nevertheless; so still that the distant cackle of the successful hen smote upon the ear but little dulled by intervening sounds. That commonest of village sights was lacking here—the public pump, with its great stone tank or trough of limpid water, and its group of gossiping pitcher-bearers; for there is no well or fountain or spring on this tall hill; cisterns of rain-water are used.

Our alpenstocks and muslin tails compelled attention, and as we moved through the village we gathered a considerable procession of little boys and girls, and so went in some state to the castle. It proved to be an extensive pile of crumbling walls, arches, and towers, massive, properly grouped for picturesque effect, weedy, grass-grown, and satisfactory. The children acted as guides; they walked us along the top of the highest walls, then took us up into a high tower and showed us a wide and beautiful landscape, made up of wavy distances of woody hills, and a nearer prospect of undulating expanses of green lowlands, on the one hand, and castle-graced crags and ridges on the other, with the shining curves of the Neckar flowing between. But the principal show, the chief pride of the children, was the ancient and empty well in the grass-grown court of the castle. Its massive stone curb stands up three or four feet above-ground, and is whole and uninjured. The children said that in the Middle Ages this well was four hundred feet deep, and furnished all the village with an abundant supply of water, in war and peace. They said that in the old day its bottom was below the level of the Neckar, hence the water-supply was inexhaustible.

But there were some who believed it had never been a well at all, and was never deeper than it is now—eighty feet; that at that depth a subterranean passage branched from it and descended gradually to a remote place in the valley, where it opened into somebody's cellar or other hidden recess, and that the secret of this locality is now lost. Those who hold this belief say that herein lies the explanation that Dilsberg, besieged by Tilly and many a soldier before him, was never taken: after the longest and closest sieges the besiegers were astonished to perceive that the besieged were as fat and hearty as ever, and were well furnished with munitions of war—therefore it must be that the Dilsbergers had been bringing these things in through the subterranean passage all the time.

The children said that there was in truth a subterranean outlet down there, and they would prove it. So they set a great truss of straw on fire and threw it down the well, while we leaned on the curb and watched the glowing mass descend. It struck bottom and gradually burned out. No smoke came up. The children clapped their hands and said:

"You see! Nothing makes so much smoke as burning straw—now where did the smoke go to, if there is no subterranean outlet?"

So it seemed quite evident that the subterranean outlet indeed existed. But the finest thing within the ruin's limits was a noble linden, which the children said was four hundred years old, and no doubt it was. It had a mighty trunk and a mighty spread of limb and foliage. The limbs near the ground were nearly the thickness of a barrel.

That tree had witnessed the assaults of men in mail—how remote such a time seems, and how ungraspable is the fact that real men ever did fight in real armor!—and it had seen the time when these broken arches and crumbling battlements were a trim and strong and stately fortress, fluttering its gay banners in the sun, and peopled with vigorous humanity—how impossibly long ago that seems!—and here it stands yet, and possibly may still be standing here, sunning itself and dreaming its historical dreams, when today shall have been joined to the days called "ancient."

Well, we sat down under the tree to smoke, and the captain delivered himself of his legend:

THE LEGEND OF DILSBERG CASTLE

It was to this effect. In the old times there was once a great company assembled at the castle, and festivity ran high. Of course there was a haunted chamber in the castle, and one day the talk fell upon that. It was said that whoever slept in it would not wake again for fifty years. Now when a young knight named Conrad von Geisberg heard this, he said that if the castle were his he would destroy that chamber, so that no foolish person might have the chance to bring so dreadful a misfortune upon himself and afflict such as loved him with the memory of it. Straightway, the company privately laid their heads together to contrive some way to get this superstitious young man to sleep in that chamber.

And they succeeded—in this way. They persuaded his betrothed, a lovely mischievous young creature, niece of the lord of the castle, to help them in their plot. She presently took him aside and had speech with him. She used all her persuasions, but could not shake him;

he said his belief was firm, that if he should sleep there he would wake no more for fifty years, and it made him shudder to think of it. Catharina began to weep. This was a better argument; Conrad could not hold out against it. He yielded and said she should have her wish if she would only smile and be happy again. She flung her arms about his neck, and the kisses she gave him showed that her thankfulness and her pleasure were very real. Then she flew to tell the company her success, and the applause she received made her glad and proud she had undertaken her mission, since all alone she had accomplished what the multitude had failed in.

At midnight, that night, after the usual feasting, Conrad was taken to the haunted chamber and left there. He fell asleep, by and by.

When he awoke again and looked about him, his heart stood still with horror! The whole aspect of the chamber was changed. The walls were moldy and hung with ancient cobwebs; the curtains and beddings were rotten; the furniture was rickety and ready to fall to pieces. He sprang out of bed, but his quaking knees sunk under him and he fell to the floor.

"This is the weakness of age," he said.

He rose and sought his clothing. It was clothing no longer. The colors were gone, the garments gave way in many places while he was putting them on. He fled, shuddering, into the corridor, and along it to the great hall. Here he was met by a middle-aged stranger of a kind countenance, who stopped and gazed at him with surprise. Conrad said:

"Good sir, will you send hither the lord Ulrich?"

The stranger looked puzzled a moment, then said:

"The lord Ulrich?"

"Yes—if you will be so good."

The stranger called—"Wilhelm!" A young serving-man came, and the stranger said to him:

"Is there a lord Ulrich among the guests?"

"I know none of the name, so please your honor."

Conrad said, hesitatingly:

"I did not mean a guest, but the lord of the castle, sir."

The stranger and the servant exchanged wondering glances. Then the former said:

"I am the lord of the castle."

"Since when, sir?"

"Since the death of my father, the good lord Ulrich more than forty years ago."

Conrad sank upon a bench and covered his face with his hands while he rocked his body to and fro and moaned. The stranger said in a low voice to the servant:

"I fear me this poor old creature is mad. Call some one."

In a moment several people came, and grouped themselves about, talking in whispers. Conrad looked up and scanned the faces about him wistfully.

Then he shook his head and said, in a grieved voice:

"No, there is none among ye that I know. I am old and alone in the world. They are dead and gone these many years that cared for me. But sure, some of these aged ones I see about me can tell me some little word or two concerning them."

Several bent and tottering men and women came nearer and answered his questions about each former friend as he mentioned the names. This one they said had been dead ten years, that one twenty, another thirty. Each succeeding blow struck heavier and heavier. At last the sufferer said:

"There is one more, but I have not the courage to—O my lost Catharina!"

One of the old dames said:

"Ah, I knew her well, poor soul. A misfortune overtook her lover, and she died of sorrow nearly fifty years ago. She lieth under the linden tree without the court."

Conrad bowed his head and said:

"Ah, why did I ever wake! And so she died of grief for me, poor child. So young, so sweet, so good! She never wittingly did a hurtful thing in all the little summer of her life. Her loving debt shall be repaid—for I will die of grief for her."

His head drooped upon his breast. In the moment there was a wild burst of joyous laughter, a pair of round young arms were flung about Conrad's neck and a sweet voice cried:

"There, Conrad mine, thy kind words kill me—the farce shall go no further! Look up, and laugh with us—'twas all a jest!"

And he did look up, and gazed, in a dazed wonderment—for the disguises were stripped away, and the aged men and women were bright and young and gay again. Catharina's happy tongue ran on:

"'Twas a marvelous jest, and bravely carried out. They gave you a heavy sleeping-draught before you went to bed, and in the night they bore you to a ruined chamber where all had fallen to decay, and placed these rags of clothing by you. And when your sleep was spent and you came forth, two strangers, well instructed in their parts, were here to meet you; and all we, your friends, in our disguises, were close at hand, to see and hear, you may be sure. Ah, 'twas a gallant jest! Come, now, and make thee ready for the pleasures of the day. How real was thy misery for the moment, thou poor lad! Look up and have thy laugh, now!"

He looked up, searched the merry faces about him in a dreamy way, then sighed and said:

"I am aweary, good strangers, I pray you lead me to her grave."

All the smile vanished away, every cheek blanched, Catharina sunk to the ground in a swoon.

All day the people went about the castle with troubled faces, and communed together in undertones. A painful hush pervaded the place which had lately been so full of cheery life. Each in his turn tried to arouse Conrad out of his hallucination and bring him to himself; but all the answer any got was a meek, bewildered stare, and then the words:

"Good stranger, I have no friends, all are at rest these many years; ye speak me fair, ye mean me well, but I know ye not; I am alone and forlorn in the world—prithee lead me to her grave."

During two years Conrad spent his days, from the early morning till the night, under the linden tree, mourning over the imaginary grave of his Catharina. Catharina was the only company of the harmless madman. He was very friendly toward her because, as he said, in some ways she reminded him of his Catharina whom he had lost "fifty years ago." He often said:

"She was so gay, so happy-hearted—but you never smile; and always when you think I am not looking, you cry."

When Conrad died, they buried him under the linden, according to his directions, so that he might rest "near his poor Catharina." Then Catharina sat under the linden alone, every day and all day long, a great many years, speaking to no one, and never smiling; and at last her long repentance was rewarded with death, and she was buried by Conrad's side.

Harris pleased the captain by saying it was good legend; and pleased him further by adding:

"Now that I have seen this mighty tree, vigorous with its four hundred years, I feel a desire to believe the legend for ITS sake; so I will humor the desire, and consider that the tree really watches over those poor hearts and feels a sort of human tenderness for them."

We returned to Necharsteinach, plunged our hot heads into the trough at the town pump, and then went to the hotel and ate our trout dinner in leisurely comfort, in the garden, with the beautiful Neckar flowing at our feet, the quaint Dilsberg looming beyond, and the graceful towers and battlements of a couple of medieval castles (called the "Swallow's Nest" [1] and "The Brothers.") assisting the rugged scenery of a bend of the river down to our right. We got to sea in season to make the eight-mile run to Heidelberg before the night shut down. We sailed by the hotel in the mellow glow of sunset, and came slashing down with the mad current into the narrow passage between the dikes. I believed I could shoot the bridge myself, and I went to the forward triplet of logs and relieved the pilot of his pole and his responsibility.

1. The seeker after information is referred to Appendix E
for our captain's legend of the "Swallow's Nest" and
"The Brothers."

We went tearing along in a most exhilarating way, and I performed the delicate duties of my office very well indeed for a first attempt; but perceiving, presently, that I really was going to shoot the bridge itself instead of the archway under it, I judiciously stepped ashore. The next moment I had my long-coveted desire: I saw a raft wrecked. It hit the pier in the center and went all to smash and scatteration like a box of matches struck by lightning.

I was the only one of our party who saw this grand sight; the others were attitudinizing, for the benefit of the long rank of young ladies who were promenading on the bank, and so they lost it. But I helped to fish them out of the river, down below the bridge, and then described it to them as well as I could.

They were not interested, though. They said they were wet and felt ridiculous and did not care anything for descriptions of scenery. The young ladies, and other people, crowded around and showed a great deal of sympathy, but that did not help matters; for my friends said they did not want sympathy, they wanted a back alley and solitude.

CHAPTER XX
[My Precious, Priceless Tear-Jug]

Next morning brought good news—our trunks had arrived from Hamburg at last. Let this be a warning to the reader. The Germans are very conscientious, and this trait makes them very particular. Therefore if you tell a German you want a thing done immediately, he takes you at your word; he thinks you mean what you say; so he does that thing immediately—according to his idea of immediately—which is about a week; that is, it is a week if it refers to the building of a garment, or it is an hour and a half if it refers to the cooking of a trout. Very well; if you tell a German to send your trunk to you by "slow freight," he takes you at your word; he sends it by "slow freight," and you cannot imagine how long you will go on enlarging your admiration of the expressiveness of that phrase in the German tongue, before you get that trunk. The hair on my trunk was soft and thick and youthful, when I got it ready for shipment in Hamburg; it was baldheaded when it reached Heidelberg. However, it was still sound, that was a comfort, it was not battered in the least; the baggagemen seemed to be conscientiously careful, in Germany, of the baggage entrusted to their hands. There was nothing now in the way of our departure, therefore we set about our preparations.

Naturally my chief solicitude was about my collection of Ceramics. Of course I could not take it with me, that would be inconvenient, and dangerous besides. I took advice, but the best brick-a-brackers were divided as to the wisest course to pursue; some said pack the collection and warehouse it; others said try to get it into the Grand Ducal Museum at Mannheim for safe keeping. So I divided the collection, and followed the advice of both parties. I set aside, for the Museum, those articles which were the most frail and precious.

Among these was my Etruscan tear-jug. I have made a little sketch of it here; that thing creeping up the side is not a bug, it is a hole. I bought this tear-jug of a dealer in antiquities for four hundred and fifty dollars. It is very rare. The man said the Etruscans used to keep tears or something in these things, and that it was very hard to get hold of a broken one, now.

I also set aside my Henri II. plate. See sketch from my pencil; it is in the main correct, though I think I have foreshortened one end of it a little too much, perhaps. This is very fine and rare; the shape is exceedingly beautiful and unusual. It has wonderful decorations on it, but I am not able to reproduce them. It cost more than the tear-jug, as the dealer said there was not another plate just like it in the world. He said there was much false Henri II ware around, but that the genuineness of this piece was unquestionable.

He showed me its pedigree, or its history, if you please; it was a document which traced this plate's movements all the way down from its birth—showed who bought it, from whom, and what he paid for it—from the first buyer down to me, whereby I saw that it had gone steadily up from thirty-five cents to seven hundred dollars. He said that the whole Ceramic world would be informed that it was now in my possession and would make a note of it, with the price paid. [Figure 8]

There were Masters in those days, but, alas—it is not so now. Of course the main preciousness of this piece lies in its color; it is that old sensuous, pervading, ramifying, interpolating, transboreal blue which is the despair of modern art. The little sketch which I have made of this gem cannot and does not do it justice, since I have been obliged to leave out the color. But I've got the expression, though.

However, I must not be frittering away the reader's time with these details. I did not intend to go into any detail at all, at first, but it is the failing of the true ceramiker, or the true devotee in any department of brick-a-brackery, that once he gets his tongue or his pen started on his darling theme, he cannot well stop until he drops from exhaustion. He has no more sense of the flight of time than has any other lover when talking of his sweetheart. The very "marks" on the bottom of a piece of rare crockery are able to throw me into a gibbering ecstasy; and I could forsake a drowning relative to help dispute about whether the stopple of a departed Buon Retiro scent-bottle was genuine or spurious.

Many people say that for a male person, bric-a-brac hunting is about as robust a business as making doll-clothes, or decorating Japanese pots with decalcomania butterflies would be, and these people fling mud at the elegant Englishman, Byng, who wrote a book called THE BRIC-A-BRAC HUNTER, and make fun of him for chasing around after what they choose to call "his despicable trifles"; and for "gushing" over these trifles; and for exhibiting his "deep infantile delight" in what they call his "tuppenny collection of beggarly trivialities"; and for beginning his book with a picture of himself seated, in a "sappy, self-complacent attitude, in the midst of his poor little ridiculous bric-a-brac junk shop."

It is easy to say these things; it is easy to revile us, easy to despise us; therefore, let these people rail on; they cannot feel as Byng and I feel—it is their loss, not ours. For my part I am content to be a brick-a-bracker and a ceramiker—more, I am proud to be so named. I am proud to know that I lose my reason as immediately in the presence of a rare jug with an illustrious mark on the bottom of it, as if I had just emptied that jug. Very well; I packed and stored a part of my collection, and the rest of it I placed in the care of the Grand Ducal Museum in Mannheim, by permission. My Old Blue China Cat remains there yet. I presented it to that excellent institution.

I had but one misfortune with my things. An egg which I had kept back from breakfast that morning, was broken in packing. It was a great pity. I had shown it to the best connoisseurs in Heidelberg, and they all said it was an antique. We spent a day or two in farewell visits, and then left for Baden-Baden. We had a pleasant trip to it, for the Rhine valley is always lovely. The only trouble was that the trip was too short. If I remember rightly it only occupied a couple of hours, therefore I judge that the distance was very little, if any, over fifty miles. We quitted the train at Oos, and walked the entire remaining distance to Baden-Baden, with the exception of a lift of less than an hour which we got on a passing wagon, the weather being exhaustingly warm. We came into town on foot.

One of the first persons we encountered, as we walked up the street, was the Rev. Mr. ———, an old friend from America—a lucky encounter, indeed, for his is a most gentle, refined, and sensitive nature, and his company and companionship are a genuine refreshment. We knew he had been in Europe some time, but were not at all expecting to run across him. Both parties burst forth into loving enthusiasms, and Rev. Mr. ——— said:

"I have got a brimful reservoir of talk to pour out on you, and an empty one ready and thirsting to receive what you have got; we will sit up till midnight and have a good satisfying interchange, for I leave here early in the morning." We agreed to that, of course.

I had been vaguely conscious, for a while, of a person who was walking in the street abreast of us; I had glanced furtively at him once or twice, and noticed that he was a fine, large, vigorous young fellow, with an open, independent countenance, faintly shaded with a pale and even almost imperceptible crop of early down, and that he was clothed from head to heel in cool and enviable snow-white linen. I thought I had also noticed that his head had a sort of listening tilt to it. Now about this time the Rev. Mr. ——— said:

"The sidewalk is hardly wide enough for three, so I will walk behind; but keep the talk going, keep the talk going, there's no time to lose, and you may be sure I will do my share." He ranged himself behind us, and straightway that stately snow-white young fellow closed up to the sidewalk alongside him, fetched him a cordial slap on the shoulder with his broad palm, and sung out with a hearty cheeriness:

"AMERICANS for two-and-a-half and the money up! HEY?"

The Reverend winced, but said mildly:

"Yes—we are Americans."

"Lord love you, you can just bet that's what _I_ am, every time! Put it there!"

He held out his Sahara of his palm, and the Reverend laid his diminutive hand in it, and got so cordial a shake that we heard his glove burst under it.

"Say, didn't I put you up right?"

"Oh, yes."

"Sho! I spotted you for MY kind the minute I heard your clack. You been over here long?"

"About four months. Have you been over long?"

"LONG? Well, I should say so! Going on two YEARS, by geeminy! Say, are you homesick?"

"No, I can't say that I am. Are you?"

"Oh, HELL, yes!" This with immense enthusiasm.

The Reverend shrunk a little, in his clothes, and we were aware, rather by instinct than otherwise, that he was throwing out signals of distress to us; but we did not interfere or try to succor him, for we were quite happy.

The young fellow hooked his arm into the Reverend's, now, with the confiding and grateful air of a waif who has been longing for a friend, and a sympathetic ear, and a chance to lisp once more the sweet accents of the mother-tongue—and then he limbered up the muscles of his mouth and turned himself loose—and with such a relish! Some of his words were not Sunday-school words, so I am obliged to put blanks where they occur.

"Yes indeedy! If _I_ ain't an American there AIN'T any Americans, that's all. And when I heard you fellows gassing away in the good old American language, I'm ——— if it wasn't all I could do to keep from hugging you! My tongue's all warped with trying to curl it around these ——— forsaken wind-galled nine-jointed German words here; now I TELL you it's awful good to lay it over a Christian word once more and kind of let the old taste soak it. I'm from western New York. My name is Cholley Adams. I'm a student, you know. Been here going on two years. I'm learning to be a horse-doctor! I LIKE that part of it, you know, but ———these people, they won't learn a fellow in his own language, they make him learn in German; so before I could tackle the horse-doctoring I had to tackle this miserable language.

"First off, I thought it would certainly give me the botts, but I don't mind now. I've got it where the hair's short, I think; and dontchuknow, they made me learn Latin, too. Now between you and me, I wouldn't give a ———for all the Latin that was ever jabbered; and the first thing _I_ calculate to do when I get through, is to just sit down and forget it. 'Twon't take me long, and I don't mind the time, anyway. And I tell you what! the difference between school-teaching over yonder and school-teaching over here—sho! WE don't know anything about it! Here you've got to peg and peg and peg and there just ain't any let-up—and what you learn here, you've got to KNOW, dontchuknow —or else you'll have one of these ——— spavined, spectacles, ring-boned, knock-kneed old professors in your hair. I've been here long ENOUGH, and I'm getting blessed tired of it, mind I TELL you. The old man wrote me that he was coming over in June, and said he'd take me home in August, whether I was done with my education or not, but durn him, he didn't come; never said why; just sent me a hamper of Sunday-school books, and told me to be good, and hold on a while. I don't take to Sunday-school books, dontchuknow—I don't hanker after them when I can get pie—but I READ them, anyway, because whatever the old man tells me to do, that's the thing that I'm a-going to DO, or tear something, you know. I buckled in and read all those books, because he wanted me to; but that kind of thing don't excite ME, I like something HEARTY. But I'm awful homesick. I'm homesick from ear-socket to crupper, and from crupper to hock-joint; but it ain't any use, I've got to stay here, till the old man drops the rag and give the word—yes, SIR, right here in this ——— country I've got to linger till the old man says COME!—and you bet your bottom dollar, Johnny, it AIN'T just as easy as it is for a cat to have twins!"

At the end of this profane and cordial explosion he fetched a prodigious "WHOOSH!" to relieve his lungs and make recognition of the heat, and then he straightway dived into his narrative again for "Johnny's" benefit, beginning, "Well, ———it ain't any use talking, some of those old American words DO have a kind of a bully swing to them; a man can EXPRESS himself with 'em—a man can get at what he wants to SAY, dontchuknow."

When we reached our hotel and it seemed that he was about to lose the Reverend, he showed so much sorrow, and begged so hard and so earnestly that the Reverend's heart was not hard enough to hold out against the pleadings—so he went away with the parent-honoring student, like a right Christian, and took supper with him in his lodgings, and sat in the surf-beat of his slang and profanity till near midnight, and then left him—left him pretty well talked out, but grateful "clear down to his frogs," as he expressed it. The Reverend said it had transpired during the interview that "Cholley" Adams's father was an extensive dealer in horses in western New York; this accounted for Cholley's choice of a profession. The Reverend brought away a pretty high opinion of Cholley as a manly young fellow, with stuff in him for a useful citizen; he considered him rather a rough gem, but a gem, nevertheless.

CHAPTER XXI
[Insolent Shopkeepers and Gabbling Americans]

Baden-Baden sits in the lap of the hills, and the natural and artificial beauties of the surroundings are combined effectively and charmingly. The level strip of ground which stretches through and beyond the town is laid out in handsome pleasure grounds, shaded by noble trees and adorned at intervals with lofty and sparkling fountain-jets. Thrice a day a fine band makes music in the public promenade before the Conversation House, and in the afternoon and evening that locality is populous with fashionably dressed people of both sexes, who march back and forth past the great music-stand and look very much bored, though they make a show of feeling otherwise. It seems like a rather aimless and stupid existence. A good many of these people are there for a real purpose, however; they are racked with rheumatism, and they are there to stew it out in the hot baths. These invalids looked melancholy enough, limping about on their canes and crutches, and apparently brooding over all sorts of cheerless things. People say that Germany, with her damp stone houses, is the home of rheumatism. If that is so, Providence must have foreseen that it would be so, and therefore filled the land with the healing baths. Perhaps no other country is so generously supplied with medicinal springs as Germany. Some of these baths are good for one ailment, some for another; and again, peculiar ailments are conquered by combining the individual virtues of several different baths. For instance, for some forms of disease, the patient drinks the native hot water of Baden-Baden, with a spoonful of salt from the Carlsbad springs dissolved in it. That is not a dose to be forgotten right away.

They don't SELL this hot water; no, you go into the great Trinkhalle, and stand around, first on one foot and then on the other, while two or three young girls sit pottering at some sort of ladylike sewing-work in your neighborhood and can't seem to see you — polite as three-dollar clerks in government offices.

By and by one of these rises painfully, and "stretches"—stretches fists and body heavenward till she raises her heels from the floor, at the same time refreshing herself with a yawn of such comprehensiveness that the bulk of her face disappears behind her upper lip and one is able to see how she is constructed inside—then she slowly closes her cavern, brings down her fists and her heels, comes languidly forward, contemplates you contemptuously, draws you a glass of hot water and sets it down where you can get it by reaching for it. You take it and say:

"How much?"—and she returns you, with elaborate indifference, a beggar's answer:
"NACH BELIEBE." (what you please.)

This thing of using the common beggar's trick and the common beggar's shibboleth to put you on your liberality when you were expecting a simple straightforward commercial transaction, adds a little to your prospering sense of irritation. You ignore her reply, and ask again:

"How much?"

—and she calmly, indifferently, repeats:
"NACH BELIEBE."

You are getting angry, but you are trying not to show it; you resolve to keep on asking your question till she changes her answer, or at least her annoyingly indifferent manner. Therefore, if your case be like mine, you two fools stand there, and without perceptible emotion of any kind, or any emphasis on any syllable, you look blandly into each other's eyes, and hold the following idiotic conversation:

"How much?"
"NACH BELIEBE."
"How much?"
"NACH BELIEBE."
"How much?"
"NACH BELIEBE."
"How much?"
"NACH BELIEBE."
"How much?"
"NACH BELIEBE."
"How much?"
"NACH BELIEBE."

I do not know what another person would have done, but at this point I gave up; that cast-iron indifference, that tranquil contemptuousness, conquered me, and I struck my colors. Now I knew she was used to receiving about a penny from manly people who care nothing about the opinions of scullery-maids, and about tuppence from moral cowards; but I laid a silver twenty-five cent piece within her reach and tried to shrivel her up with this sarcastic speech:

"If it isn't enough, will you stoop sufficiently from your official dignity to say so?"

She did not shrivel. Without deigning to look at me at all, she languidly lifted the coin and bit it!—to see if it was good. Then she turned her back and placidly waddled to her former roost again, tossing the money into an open till as she went along. She was victor to the last, you see.

I have enlarged upon the ways of this girl because they are typical; her manners are the manners of a goodly number of the Baden-Baden shopkeepers. The shopkeeper there swindles you if he can, and insults you whether he succeeds in swindling you or not. The keepers of baths also take great and patient pains to insult you. The frowsy woman who sat at the desk in the lobby of the great Friederichsbad and sold bath tickets, not only insulted me twice every day, with rigid fidelity to her great trust, but she took trouble enough to cheat me out of a shilling, one day, to have fairly entitled her to ten. Baden-Baden's splendid gamblers are gone, only her microscopic knaves remain.

An English gentleman who had been living there several years, said:

"If you could disguise your nationality, you would not find any insolence here. These shopkeepers detest the English and despise the Americans; they are rude to both, more especially to ladies of your nationality and mine. If these go shopping without a gentleman or a man-servant, they are tolerably sure to be subjected to petty insolences—insolences of manner and tone, rather than word, though words that are hard to bear are not always wanting. I know of an instance where a shopkeeper tossed a coin back to an American lady with the remark, snappishly uttered, 'We don't take French money here.' And I know of a case where an English lady said to one of these shopkeepers, 'Don't you think you ask too much for this article?' and he replied with the question, 'Do you think you are obliged to buy it?' However, these people are not impolite to Russians or Germans. And as to rank, they worship that, for they have long been used to generals and nobles. If you wish to see what abysses servility can descend, present yourself before a Baden-Baden shopkeeper in the character of a Russian prince."

It is an inane town, filled with sham, and petty fraud, and snobbery, but the baths are good. I spoke with many people, and they were all agreed in that. I had the twinges of rheumatism unceasingly during three years, but the last one departed after a fortnight's bathing there, and I have never had one since. I fully believe I left my rheumatism in Baden-Baden. Baden-Baden is welcome to it. It was little, but it was all I had to give. I would have preferred to leave something that was catching, but it was not in my power.

There are several hot springs there, and during two thousand years they have poured forth a never-diminishing abundance of the healing water. This water is conducted in pipe to the numerous bath-houses, and is reduced to an endurable temperature by the addition of cold water. The new Friederichsbad is a very large and beautiful building, and in it one may have any sort of bath that has ever been invented, and with all the additions of herbs and drugs that his ailment may need or that the physician of the establishment may consider a useful thing to put into the water. You go there, enter the great door, get a bow graduated to your style and clothes from the gorgeous portier, and a bath ticket and an insult from the frowsy woman for a quarter; she strikes a bell and a serving-man conducts you down a long hall and shuts you into a commodious room which has a washstand, a mirror, a bootjack, and a sofa in it, and there you undress at your leisure.

The room is divided by a great curtain; you draw this curtain aside, and find a large white marble bathtub, with its rim sunk to the level of the floor, and with three white marble steps leading down to it. This tub is full of water which is as clear as crystal, and is tempered to 28 degrees Re'aumur (about 95 degrees Fahrenheit). Sunk into the floor, by the tub, is a covered copper box which contains some warm towels and a sheet. You look fully as white as an angel when you are stretched out in that limpid bath. You remain in it ten minutes, the first time, and afterward increase the duration from day to day, till you reach twenty-five or thirty minutes. There you stop. The appointments of the place are so luxurious, the benefit so marked, the price so moderate, and the insults so sure, that you very soon find yourself adoring the Friederichsbad and infesting it.

We had a plain, simple, unpretending, good hotel, in Baden-Baden—the Hôtel de France—and alongside my room I had a giggling, cackling, chattering family who always went to bed just two hours after me and always got up two hours ahead of me. But this is common in German hotels; the people generally go to bed long after eleven and get up long before eight. The partitions convey sound like a drum-head, and everybody knows it; but no matter, a German family who are all kindness and consideration in the daytime make apparently no effort to moderate their noises for your benefit at night. They will sing, laugh, and talk loudly, and bang furniture around in a most pitiless way. If you knock on your wall appealingly, they will quiet down and discuss the matter softly among themselves for a moment—then, like the mice, they fall to persecuting you again, and as vigorously as before. They keep cruelly late and early hours, for such noisy folk.

Of course, when one begins to find fault with foreign people's ways, he is very likely to get a reminder to look nearer home, before he gets far with it. I open my note-book to see if I can find some more information of a valuable nature about Baden-Baden, and the first thing I fall upon is this:

"BADEN-BADEN (no date). Lot of vociferous Americans at breakfast this morning. Talking AT everybody, while pretending to talk among themselves. On their first travels, manifestly. Showing off. The usual signs—airy, easy-going references to grand distances and foreign places. 'Well GOOD-by, old fellow—if I don't run across you in Italy, you hunt me up in London before you sail.'"

The next item which I find in my note-book is this one:

"The fact that a band of 6,000 Indians are now murdering our frontiersmen at their impudent leisure, and that we are only able to send 1,200 soldiers against them, is utilized here to discourage emigration to America. The common people think the Indians are in New Jersey."

This is a new and peculiar argument against keeping our army down to a ridiculous figure in the matter of numbers. It is rather a striking one, too. I have not distorted the truth in saying that the facts in the above item, about the army and the Indians, are made use of to discourage emigration to America. That the common people should be rather foggy in their geography, and foggy as to the location of the Indians, is a matter for amusement, maybe, but not of surprise.

There is an interesting old cemetery in Baden-Baden, and we spent several pleasant hours in wandering through it and spelling out the inscriptions on the aged tombstones. Apparently after a man has laid there a century or two, and has had a good many people buried on top of him, it is considered that his tombstone is not needed by him any longer. I judge so from the fact that hundreds of old gravestones have been removed from the graves and placed against the inner walls of the cemetery. What artists they had in the old times! They chiseled angels and cherubs and devils and skeletons on the tombstones in the most lavish and generous way—as to supply—but curiously grotesque and outlandish as to form. It is not always easy to tell which of the figures belong among the blest and which of them among the opposite party. But there was an inscription, in French, on one of those old stones, which was quaint and pretty, and was plainly not the work of any other than a poet. It was to this effect:

Here Reposes in God, Caroline de Clery, a Religieuse of St. Denis aged 83 years—and blind. The light was restored to her in Baden the 5th of January, 1839

We made several excursions on foot to the neighboring villages, over winding and beautiful roads and through enchanting woodland scenery. The woods and roads were similar to those at Heidelberg, but not so bewitching. I suppose that roads and woods which are up to the Heidelberg mark are rare in the world.

Once we wandered clear away to La Favorita Palace, which is several miles from Baden-Baden. The grounds about the palace were fine; the palace was a curiosity. It was built by a Margravine in 1725, and remains as she left it at her death. We wandered through a great many of its rooms, and they all had striking peculiarities of decoration. For instance, the walls of one room were pretty completely covered with small pictures of the Margravine in all conceivable varieties of fanciful costumes, some of them male.

The walls of another room were covered with grotesquely and elaborately figured hand-wrought tapestry. The musty ancient beds remained in the chambers, and their quilts and curtains and canopies were decorated with curious handwork, and the walls and ceilings frescoed with historical and mythological scenes in glaring colors. There was enough crazy and rotten rubbish in the building to make a true brick-a-bracker green with envy. A painting in the dining-hall verged upon the indelicate—but then the Margravine was herself a trifle indelicate.

It is in every way a wildly and picturesquely decorated house, and brimful of interest as a reflection of the character and tastes of that rude bygone time.

In the grounds, a few rods from the palace, stands the Margravine's chapel, just as she left it—a coarse wooden structure, wholly barren of ornament. It is said that the Margravine would give herself up to debauchery and exceedingly fast living for several months at a time, and then retire to this miserable wooden den and spend a few months in repenting and getting ready for another good time. She was a devoted Catholic, and was perhaps quite a model sort of a Christian as Christians went then, in high life.

Tradition says she spent the last two years of her life in the strange den I have been speaking of, after having indulged herself in one final, triumphant, and satisfying spree. She shut herself up there, without company, and without even a servant, and so abjured and forsook the world. In her little bit of a kitchen she did her own cooking; she wore a hair shirt next the skin, and castigated herself with whips—these aids to grace are exhibited there yet. She prayed and told her beads, in another little room, before a waxen Virgin niched in a little box against the wall; she bedded herself like a slave.

In another small room is an unpainted wooden table, and behind it sit half-life-size waxen figures of the Holy Family, made by the very worst artist that ever lived, perhaps, and clothed in gaudy, flimsy drapery. [1] The margravine used to bring her meals to this table and DINE WITH THE HOLY FAMILY. What an idea that was! What a grisly spectacle it must have been! Imagine it: Those rigid, shock-headed figures, with corpsy complexions and fish glass eyes, occupying one side of the table in the constrained attitudes and dead fixedness that distinguish all men that are born of wax, and this wrinkled, smoldering old fire-eater occupying the other side, mumbling her prayers and munching her sausages in the ghostly stillness and shadowy indistinctness of a winter twilight. It makes one feel crawly even to think of it.

[1] The Savior was represented as a lad of about fifteen years of age. This figure had lost one eye.

In this sordid place, and clothed, bedded, and fed like a pauper, this strange princess lived and worshiped during two years, and in it she died. Two or three hundred years ago, this would have made the poor den holy ground; and the church would have set up a miracle-factory there and made plenty of money out of it. The den could be moved into some portions of France and made a good property even now.

Printed in the USA
CPSIA information can be obtained
at www.ICGtesting.com
LVHW012217200124
769368LV00005B/287